THE FEMALE BUDDHA

JANEESH JAJIKALAYAM

Title   :   The Female Buddha

Author   :   Janeesh Jajikalayam

Edition   :   1st (January, 2024)

ISBN   :   9788196942595

Published by

TANEESHA
PUBLISHERS

Regd. Add.: 254, Khuriyakhatta No. 10, Bindukhatta,
Lalkuan, Nainital - 262402, Uttarakhand, India
Website : www.taneeshapublishers.in
E-mail : taneeshapublishers@gmail.com
Phone : +91 845481 2712, +91 976041 7980

Printed by :
Manipal Technologies Limited, Bengaluru - 560001, Karnataka

COPYRIGHT NOTICE

Dedicated to

M.J Radhakrishnan

contents

Preface

Mother Tara Devi create the beauty of culture and art and there by ensure the beauty of writing and reading in life. My first love has no starting so it is never end. Thich nhat hanh book cultivating the mind of love talk to me "Your first love is not your first love it is just love. It is one with everything. I read several books by Tara Devi. I think about my own first love. I every time recall that experience and look at it calmly and deeply into my first love and try to its true face. My first love is still present, always with me here. Continuing to shape my life. When I met her I had not seen the image of Buddha Tara Devi. Our meeting not have been possible. She had been practicing her education. The moment I invited to see she shifted she looked the way she seems spoke she was quit and busy she said she will call me. True love started. I tried to writing I went in to Bodhgaya has to see Buddha. And again visit Tara Devi. I heard her voice in beside me I was alone on the temple. I saw her again standing infront of the temple. She didn't met me. One day I heard her voice in my mobile I talk to her about cultivating the mind of love. I invited she visit Tara

Devi spring comes slowly and quietly every time love is stronger than our determination the wonderful sounds of birds the breeze of spring in its song express my love my soul is free the spring has really come she will come back near Buddha. She is real life present moment.

The story of Tara Devi might be said to have began with a loss of innocence. Seek no intimacy with the beloved and also not with the unloved for not to see the beloved and to see the loved both are painful. Worship of Tara is a meditation. It is a way of life. It encompasses all aspects of life. Physical, Mental, Social that create us happy we need a healthy body and a focused mind. Tara worship makes that possible. We also need emotional satisfaction in social relationships and spiritual pursuits worship of Tara teach us how to go and achieving these- Tara protect relational losses, death, rejection, separation, There are 21 aspects of Tara in all.

Tara worship is universal in modern age. The Buddha himself never put anything in writing his faithful disciples and their disciples much after the Buddha's parinirvana truly recorded their collections of his thought and life. Tibetan script was directly adapted from Indian Devanagari script. The temple of Tara enshrines 21 statues that are the manifestation of the goddess Tara. Wisdom, happiness increases by visiting Tara. Statues offer a very powerful means to connect ordinary being with the blessings of the of the protectors and saviours of the world.

Tara is known as the mother of mercy and compassion. Tara is considered the mother of Tibetan people and the mother of the Buddha's.

Meditation upon female Buddha Tara can open our heart to loving kindness and compassion. Tara also helps liberate me from fears, delusions and ignorance. Tara protect and support me from all the unfortunate circumstances and fears.

This Book relates to all the importance of female Buddha Tara. This writings characterizes the spirit of Buddhism effectively can be found in the welcome it has received through out the Buddhist world. It sketches the picture of female Buddha Tara instead of creating sentiments of friendship and worship. Tara dispels the illusions of our mind and redeems us from the terror of death.

Tara view the concept of Truth as basic. Tara create good interpersonal relationship with human nature. Tara is the teacher she guide us to move forward. Tara teach us insight into the true nature of reality. Theravada Tradition, Vipasana, Samatha as two meditation techniques and there by ensure four stages of enlightenment Sotapanna, Sukadayami, Anagami and Arhat.

CHAPTER 1

FEMALE BUDDHA

The Bodhisattva is also described as someone who is still subject to birth illness death, sorrow defilement and delusion. According to walpola Rahula. But the fact is that the Theravadha and Mahayana unanimously accept the Bodhisattva ideal as the highest. Although the Teravadha holds that anybody can be Bodhisattva, It does not stipulate or insist that all must be Bodhisattva which is considered not practical.

When Mahayana sutras present stories of Buddha's and bodhisattvas first arising of the thought of attaining Buddha hood they invariably depict it as taking place in the presence of a Buddha.

Modern Buddhism implies that women is powerful and creative she is the mother of human kind she may also life giving force of fecundity as a positive energy. Buddhism inherited the world.

Mythological structure in which tension existed between the material aspect and the destructive aspect.

According to Shakyamuni " the establishment of the male principle in equal measure with the female principle is the natural order of things. They should never exist in a mutually exclusive relationship. They should not be an emphasis on one of the expense of the other for both are indispensable will the establishment of the true self be a fact of reality for both men and women.

The founder of Buddhism Goutama Buddha permitted women to join his monastic community and fully participate in it. The appearance of female Buddha's can be found in Vajrayana practice in Buddhism. Vajrayana Buddhism also recognizes many female yogini practitioners as achieving the full enlightenment of Buddha.

Goutami step mother of the Buddha, yasodhara Buddha's wife became a nun and Arhat. Buddhamtira, emperor Asoka etc. known as the women in Buddhist influential Era.

Once Buddha left his home at night for enlightment without lefting sleeping Yashodhara know about him. When Buddha visited Yasodhara did not go to see her former husband but for self she thought " Surely if I have gained any virtue at all the Lord will come to my presence" Some time after her son Rahula became a monk, yasodhara also entered the order of monks and Nuns as an Arhat. She was ordained as Bhikkhuni with the five hundred women following mahaprajapati Goutami. Today women desire equal status and full participation in the universe. Mother God Tara stories, images and ideals absorbed by members of a culture are potent forces. Which can give power and dignity to women. All research in human culture must right fully study Tara. The Tales and myths are restructure the importance of women in universe. Tara worship create sexual equality and positive energy to men and women and their degree of social acceptability.

The international federation of Gynaecology and obstetrics has stated that the human right of women include their right to have control over and decide freely and responsibly on matters related to their sexuality. Equal relationships between women and men in matters of sexual relations and reproduction including full respect for the integrity of the person require mutual respect consent and shared behaviour and its consequences. The relation between religion, law and gender equality has been discussed by Vajrayanam.

Female meditation teachers are role models. As for the status of women in Buddhism. Goutami her disciples, Patacara, Wanderers, wise Women's, Teachers sisters, Wives, Old women, lovers, actress, Prostitutes, beautiful models, friends, relatives, Buddhist sisters but best of all they tell the stories of their lives. Meditating really different I carried Tara protection that they were rooting for me I could sense them may be it was in my mind and head. But I had

Bought Tara to life so vividly that goddess became my companions.

CHAPTER 2

TARA DEVI

Tara Devi is the great wisdom goddesses. The word 'Tara' is derived from the Sanskrit Tantric text meaning to cross. Tara is also known as star.

Adbutha Ramayana is a Sanskrit book Traditionally attributed to the sage Valmiki. When sati in the image of kali stew Ravana, Brahma and other deities propitiated her with hymns.

Devotees visit the God Tarakanath Temple throughout the year especially on Mondays. Pilgrims visit Tarakeswar on the occasion of Shravani mela on the month of July - August.

Ancient Tarakanath Temple is believed to be constructed in 1729 AD by Raja Bharamalka. Dudhpukur pond located north of the temple is believed to full fill the prayers of those taking a dip in it. The temple enshrines one of the jyothirlinga shrines of Lord Shiva. Temple located in the town of Tarakeswar in Hoogly district of west Bengal.

A non-popular version from kalika Purana as associates Tara with Matangi. According to this. When the Devas were defeated by the demons. Sumbha and Nisumba. Mahashakti had taken the from of Tara. Devi Tara had appeared from whom the sun had to arise and supply light and energy to Earth.

Tara has the capability to produce light, energy and heat. It lead to expansion of energy. Ma Tara created Air Flow from her breath which hit the energy bodies and led to their union.

According to Hindu Devi give rebirth to Ashobhaya. Devi request Lord Surya to stay at Ashobhaya place and provide heat, light and life sustaining energy to the earth. Sun will lead to the creation of day and height and will lead to the circle of seasons on earth. Tara Devi advises sun to leave and carry out his duties of giving life to every one.

The sun is appeared by the combined power of Tara and Akshobhya. Then the increasing source of energy inside the water started assuming the appearance of the sun.

Tara had assumed the form of goddess shodashi to provide all forms of greenery and plants to the world Devi Shodashi then placed a bamboo inside the earth and poured one drop of water from her water pot, this gave birth to all plants life and then all forest, trees plant and nature grew to keep balance in the universe according to the laws of nature.

When Mahayana sutras present stories of Buddha's and bodhisattvas first arising of the thought of attaining buddhahood, they invariably depict it as taking place in the presense of a Buddha. Tara is shown standing Bodhisatta who is in the form of a cobra coiled around Tara's matted hair. Tara wears a crown made of skulls of five meditating Buddhas.

Tara has eight forms called Ashta Tara and the names are Ekajata, Ugratara, Mahogra, Kameshwari, Chamunda, Nilasaraswathi, Vajra and Kali. Tara is known as the mother of Liberation and represents the virtues of success in also known as Paranasabari.

Paranasabari the deity of diseases, worship of which is believed to offer effective protection against disaster. Statues of Paranasabari have been found in Mangolia, Dacca, India. This is connecte the detiy with Vidya, region, Sabaras, Jvarasura, Matangi, Shitala, Vajrayogini both of these escorts are again diseases related deities. They are the destroyer of diseases.

In Hinduism, the goddess Tara is the second of the ten great educations (Dasa Mahavidyas). She is the Tantric Manifestations of Durga or Mahadevi. Kali or Parvati As the star is seen as a beautiful but perpetually self combusting thing so Tara is perceived at core as the absolute unquenchable hunger that propels all life.

Tara Devi Temple is a holy place, located 11 km away from the shimla Busstand. It is positioned amid a thick forest of oak and rhododendron and offers scenic views of the lofty Himalayas surrounding the town. The temple is very famous among tourist as the clean and fresh atmosphere here helps them relax from the day to day worries of life. It is believed that the goddess Tara Devi came all the way from Bengal to Himachal Pradesh

So this temple is dedicated to the goddess of stars. Tara Devi temple is an ideal place for a person seeking peace and tranquillity.

CHAPTER 3

Tara Devi Mantra

Meaning of Tara's Mantra OM TARE TUT-TARE SOHA, When we recite it. OM TARE means " She is the one who swiftly comes to help". Tottare means "She is the one who dispels of all my fear" and TRUE means "She is the one who fulfils all my wishes" One needs to be fully aware of the meaning of the three aspects of her mantra and be confident that she has the ability to really help with out the syllables OM at the beginning and SOHA at the and, her Mantra, Consists of three Sanskrit words that describe her Buddha activities.

TARE stands for the Tibetan name myur-ma-dpha mo and means " She is the swift heroine" myur ma means "Swift" ie she does n't hesitate and helps living being who supplicate her very fast dphamo is the femine gender for the term " hero" which means to say that she is extremely determined and courageous to help those who prayer to her.

According to venerable choje Lama a phuntsok Calligraphy by 17 th Gyalwa Karmapa ogyen Trinley Dorje. TUTTARE is the Sanskrit Term for her Tibetan name

Jigs-pa-sel ma and means " She is the one who dispels any fear that we have and we do constantly live our lives driven by fear of the one kind or another. For example wealthy people live in fear or robbers and thieves and poor people fear not being able to find a job. After a couple gives birth to an off spring, they fear that their baby will get into trouble. There are so many kinds of fear that are obstacles for instance fear of not accomplishing a goad or of not being able to finish a job. This has nothing to do with the work itself, rather it is fears that evryone has for example, if one is given medicine. When one is sick, one has fears and doubts that it will help, whether ones fear is strong or weak. It is very helpful to supplicate Arya Tara because she is able to dispel and eradicate any fear that one may have.

TRUE is the Sanskrit Term in her mantra for her Tibetan name Dod-kun-sbyin-pai- Dromla and means " She is the Liberator who fulfils all wishes". We all have wishes and experience. Obstacles while trying to achieve our aims. There fore. If we supplicate Arya Tara and ask her to help us overcome our obstacles then our wishes will be fulfilled. So She is the one who grants all wishes.

As shakti Mahabagawat, She is the one who created 1st seed from which the entire universe took birth in the form of Lord Narayana.

The legend begins with the churning of the ocean between the Devas and Asuras. Lord Shiva drank the position that was created from the churning of the ocean thus saving the world from destruction but fell unconscious under its powerful effect Mahadevi appeared as

Maa Tara and Took Shiva on her Lap. She Suckled him, the milk from her breasts. Counteracting the poison and the recovered in this process turning his throat blue and earning him epithet Nilakantha.

This story is reminiscent of the one which Shiva stops the rampaging Kali by becoming an infant. Seeing the Child, Kalis Maternal instinct come to the fore and when she was feeding him her breast milk Shiva sucked her rage out while sucking the milk in both cases, Shiva assumes the position of an infant the goddess lap.

Tara Devi is depicted as standing upon a supine Shiva in an insert or corpse like form. She is shown blue in colour wearing minimal clothing is a Tiger. Skirt. She wears a garland of several human heads have a lolling tongue and blood oozes from her month.

Tara Devi has for arms holding a sacrificial sword, a severed head or skull cup, a lotus and scissors. The Scissors symbolizes Taras ability to cut through unwanted habits thus freeing the individual for spiritual transcendence.

Some researchers believe purana sabari is another name of Tara. Tara is the only female goddess not only worshipped in india but also mangolia and Russia. Again in Buddist religion. Incidentally purana sabari is depicted as attendant of Buddist deity of same name Tara.

The goddess Tara has many Incarnations now and for into past. Her name is linked to many other Goddess from around the world. She was the star woman of the cherkokees. Tara means star in Sanskrit she became the Earth to feed her people. She was the Goddess of the Druids. The great hiss of the Druids, Tara bears her name. Her name is linked to the Tara. A group of goddess women of ancient Finland who were wise and powerful. She was worshipped by ancient Hindus as an aspect of kali. She is living goddess today to the Hindus of the most beloved deity of the Tibetan Buddists. She is very similar to Kuan yin of the chinese Buddist Tradition. She is a goddess of compassion. She is also similar to parvati of today with her many different forms, both friendly and fear some. Kali is considered to be an aspect of parvati. There is a form of the Goddess Tara in every culture. It is believed that she will assume as many forms on Earth as needed by the people. In all aspects. She loves and helps the people of the Earth in every way she can.

CHAPTER 4

TARA DEVI TEMPLES

Some people believe that eye ball of sati fell hare thus this path is called Tarapith because Bengali people named eyeball as chokharmoni and another names of moni is chocker Tara. There are two images of Tara in the sanctum. The stone image of Tara depicted as a mother suckling shiva. The Primordial image is camouflaged by three feet metal image. That the devotee normally sees. represents Tara in her fiery from with four arms. Wearing a garland of skills and a protruding tongue. Crowned with a silver crown and with flowing hair, the outer image wrapped in a sari and deeked wrapped in a sari and decked in mari gold garlands with a silver umbrella over its head. The fore head of metal image is adorned with red vermillion or Sindhur.

Tara Tarini is worshipped as the breast shrine sthana peetha and manifestations of Adi Shakti. This Temple on the Kumari Hills at the Bank of the river Rushikulya near Brahmapur city in Ganjam district Odisha India.

The Shrine is considered as one of the most revered shakti peethas and Tantra peethas. It is belived that the shrine is a shakti peetha.

This is believed to have originated from the mythological story of falling of the body parts of the corps of sati Devi. When Shiva carried it and wandered. There are 51 Shakti peethas and 26 upa peethas spread across the Indian Sub continent Sati Devi breasts are believed to have fallen here in Tara Tarini. The Shakti of the Shrine is addressed as Maa Tara Devi.

The origin of shakti peethas are related to the mythology of Dakha yaga and parvathi's self immolation. This Shrines lead to the development of Shaktism in India.

The goddess of Tara and Tarini are represented by two ancient stone statues with gold and silver ornaments. Two brass heads known as their chalanti pratima or living imagine are placed between them. At the Hill top a beautiful stone temple is the adobe of Maa. Two stones anthropomorphized by the addition of gold and silver ornaments and shapped to be seen as human faces are the main shrine of this temple which represent goddess Tara and Tarini.

The origin of Shakti or worship of the Earth as a female embodiment of power is found across many culture all over the world. In Odisha which has a high density of Tribal population.

Whose religious Practice have been assimilated into main stream Hindhu faith the worship of natural formations such as rocks, trees, trunks, rivers is wide spread among the Tribes.

The temple of Dolma enshrines 21 statues that are the manifestations of the goddess Tara. According to her enlightened intention. She displays different from to protect the immeasurable numbers of helpless being using myriad skilful means.

CHAPTER 5

TYPES OF TARA

The goddess maa Ugra Tara holding potent weapons in her hand. Maa Ugra Tara is the icon of mother Tara. Tara is very popular as Ugra Tara due to the her fierce aspect but benevolent to the adorers.

Tara is a meditation deity worshipped by practitioners of the Tibetan branch of Vajrayana. Buddism to develop certain inner qualities and to understand outer, inner and secret teachings compassion, emptiness. Loving, Kindness. Tara may more properly be understood as different aspects of the same quality as Bodhisattvas are often considered metaphors for Buddhist Virtues.

There is also recognition in some school of Buddism of twenty one Taras. A practice text entitled praises to the twenty one Taras.

Praises to the twenty one Taras is a Traditional prayer in Tibetan Buddism to the female Bodhisattva Tara.

It appears in twenty one Taras. oftering praise to Tara. The prayer is found in all four traditions of Tibettan Buddism.

Each of the twenty one emanations of Tara has her

own name and specific mantra with which she is associated oftering protection from various types of fears, harm and calamities.

The twenty one Emanations of Tara according to the Tradition of suryagupta. Kashmiri mahasiddha Surya guptha each of the 21 Tara is quite different in appearance.

The central figure Tara with two attendants khadiwani Tara, Tara of the sandalwood forest is the central or principal Tara. According to the suryagupta tradition and not counted amongst the twenty one which are considered to be her emanations She is accompanied by her two attendants marici and Ekajata. Marici appears on her right from MAM. She is yellow and holds a vajra and the branch of an asoka tree and is clothed in the attire of a peaceful deity. On Tara's left appears from Hum, black Ekajata. She holds knife and skill cup filled with blood. She has three eyes and wears tiger and elephant skins and appears wrathfully.

21 Eminations of Tara

1) Pranira Tara

Tara swift & Heroic

First of Tara according to the tradition of suryagupta. Tara the heroine, red and radiating masses of fire she has one face and eight arms. The first pair of hands, Joined at the crown hold vajra and bell. The second pair hold bow and arrow. The third hold wheel and conch and the fourth hold sword, and noose. She appears peaceful and sits in the cross - legged position. She is adorned with silks and jewel ornaments and has a back rest of moonlight her seed syllable is om on a yellow lotus and moon. The lord of her family is vairocana.

2) Candrakanititara :

Tara white as Autumn moon. White Tara with three faces white blue yellow and twelve arms. Some times seated some time standing. The first pair of hands are in the contemplative gesture. The other right hands hold khatvanga, wheel, Jewel, Vajra and garland of flowers. The other left hands hold water jug, utpala, bell, flask, and book her seed syllable is TA The lord her family is Amithaba.

3) Kankuvarna Tara

Golden coloured Tara : One a Lotus and moon from R appears yellow Tara with one face and ten arms, Her right hands hold rosary, Sword, arrow vajra and staff her left hands hold sick ribbon, noose, lotus, bell and bow. The lord her family is Ratnasambhavam.

4) Usnisavijayatara:

Tara the victorious usnisa on a lotus and moon from To appears yellow Tara with one face and four arms. Her lower right hand is in the wish granting gesture and the other holds a rosary her left hand hold water flask and club. The lord of her family is amoghasidhi.

5) Humsavardhini Tara :

Tara Proclaiming the sound of Hum. The Tara practice involves the praise of Humsavardhini protect against harmful influences. Arya humkara nandhini Tara. Proclaiming the sound of hum for subding unfavourable conditions. Fill all space, directions and realms of desire while trampling the seven worlds under her feet. She brings all and every thing under her control and persuades them to practice the dharma.

6) Trailoka Vijaya Tara

Tara Victorious over three worlds. The Tara who protects against fear of failure. She protect from unsuccessful endeavours in business farming or any other project in the outside world as well as the worry, misery and mental pain caused by attachment and anger, competitiveness. and indecision.

7) Vadipramardaka Tara:

Tara crushing Adversaries Arya padmini Tara, homage to her who by TRAT and PHAT vaniqueshes evil forces conjured by magic. Right leg bent, extended left leg trampling she destroy them completely with intense blazing fire. The Lord of this type Tara is Ratnasambhava.

8) Marasudanavisitottandu Tara.

Tara who crushes all maras and bestows supreme powers. Homage to her, the swift fear some one, Who vanquishes the most tenacious of Maras when she knits her brows on her lotus face she defeats all enemies without exception - The lord of the type is amogasiddhi.

9) Varada Tara

Granter of Boons Varada Tara, Whose fingers adorn our heart with the gesture of the sublime precious three. Adorned with a wheel striking all directions without exception with the totally of your own rays of light. The lord of the type is Amoghasidhi. This Tara radiates her light to dispeal arrogance.

10) Sokavinodana Tara

Dispeller of sorrow. The Tara who spreads bound-less joy from the sparking garland of lights on her crown with great peals of laughter from the syllables TUTTARE she brings demons and the word under her control. This Tara will helpful fill our virtous wishes, especially by instructing us on how to create the cause for happiness.

11) Jagadavasivipannibarhaṇa Tara.

Tara summoner of beings, Dispeller of misfortune. Who can summon forth. The assembly of all earth pro-tectors. By the wrathful quake of the Hung in her frown, she compleately liberates all destitute beings. The lord of the type is Rathnasambhava. Her speciality is to increase enjoyments and wealth and eliminate poverty. This can bring about success in business and improve health.

12. Mangalaloka Tara

Kalyanada Tara Auspiciously shining who grants properity and brings about auspicious circumstances. Mangalaloka Tara, who crescent moon tiara and jeweled ornaments sparkle brilliantly. Who from amitabha atop her vast stream of hair floods forth immense rays of light. The Lord of this type vairocana.

13. Paripaka Tara

Tara completely Ripening. Tara the Ripener for sub-diving Hindrances engulfed in a fire like the kalpas and who sits in the midst of a wreath of flames. Right leg strectched and left leg bent, She defeats all enemies of those who rejoice when the dharma wheel turns. The Lord of this type is Amithaba.

14. Bhrikuti Tara

Tara with a Frown for protection who strikes the earth with her palms and crushes it mightly under her feet, who by hung and her wrathful glare, Rules the beings of the seven fold worlds. The lord of the type is Amoghasiddhi.

15. Mahasanti Tara

Tara of great peace her blissful virtuous and peaceful mother, whose activity is hirvanas sphere of tranquity. By the flawless expression of SOHA and OM. She overcomes even the greatest of evils. The lord of the type is Amithaba.

16. Raganisudana Tara

Tara Distroyer of attachment. Who smashes the bodies of the enemies that imprison Joy. Illuminated by the awareness of HUNG. Arranged with a Mantra of Ten syllables. The lord of the type is Aksobya.

17. Sukhasadhana Tara

Tara Accomplish happiness for binding thieves when she stamps her foot, her seed in the form of the syllabe HUNG shakes the three worlds and mount mery, mandara and vidhya the Lord of the type is Amoghasidhi.

18. Sitavijaya Tara

Victorious Liberating one her in whose hands is placed the one who bears a deer mark in the shape of a godly lake she annuals every poison with the twice uttered TARA and the sound of PHAT.

19. Dukhadhana Tara

Tara Burner of suffering Tara served by the ruler of the host of deities by gods and kinnaras. The dazzling brightness her armer of joy pispelt all quarrels and hightmaves. The Lord this type vairocana.

20. Siddhisambhava Tara

Tara source of attainments like the full sun and moon, whose two eyes shine with blazing light by TUTTARE together with HARA recited twice she eliminates even the vilest sidness.

21. Paripurana Tara

The the perfector:

The Tara who protects against fear of death. She protects from direct and indirect attacks by opponents in the outside world that prevent one from maintaining a spiritual life as well as the inner flow of deluded thinking that creates the fear of not being able to sustain oneself. endowed with the power to perfectly pacify. Through the arrangement of the three syllables of suchness. The crowds of demons, zombies and yakshas are suppressed by TRUE the supreme mother.

Tara also embodies many of the qualities of feminine principle. She is known as the mother of mercy and compassion. She is the source the female aspect of the universe, which gives birth to warmth compassion and relief from bad Karma as experienced by ordinary beings in cyclic existence. She engenders, nourishes, smiles at the vitality of creation and has sympathy for all beings as a mother does for her children.

Tara is in fact the name of a whole class of deities. She appears in all the five colours of the jinas. There are at least ten green forms, seven white, five yellow, two blue and one red.

Tara has both peaceful and wrathful forms. Her figure shown in virtually all postures from standing to sitting, full lotus, half lotus. One leg down and both legs down. There is appavently also a reclining Tara. She has two armed forms four four arms eight arms, twelve arms and Getty even mentions a Tibetan painting showing a standing Tara with one thousand heads and arms ghosh lists seventy six diatinct forms of Tara and Tradition Tell us there are one hundred and eight name for her.

Tara Sadana

Tara is meditational peity. Many of the Tara sadana are seen as beginning practices with in the world of Vajrayana buddusm by reciting her mantra and visualizing her form in front or on the head of the adept one is opening to her energies of compassion and wisdom. After a period of time the practitioner shares in some of these qualities becomes inbued with her being and all it represents. This occurs in the completion stage of the practice. This part of the sadana then is preparing the practioner to be able to confront the dissolution of one's self at death and ultimately be able to approach through various stages of meditation upon emptiness. The realization of ultimate truth as a vast display of emptiness.

The end results of doing Tara practices are many. The preparations are of two types external and internal. The external preparations consist of cleaning the meditation room, setting up a shrine with images of buddha and Green Tara and setting out a beautiful arrangements of offerings. We can use water to represent nectar for drinking water for bathing the feet and perfume. For the remaining offerings flowers incense light and pure food. If possible we should set out the actual substances.

Tara as a Yidam she is seen as having as much reality as any other phenomena appeared through the mind. By reeiting her mantra and visualizing her from in front.

Tara sadana reduces the forces of delusion in the forms of negative karma, sickness, afflictions of kleshas and other obstacles and obscuration's. Tara meditation is a means of seeing the true face of your mind. devoid of any trace of delusion.

White Tara meditation represents the enlightened activity of pacifying for example our coming sickness, causes of untimely death and obstacles to success in ones life's or ones practice.

yellow Tara sadana represents the enlightened activity of increasing the positive qualities conclusive to a long life, peace happiness and success in one Dharma practice she increases wealth and intelligence.

Red Tara represents the enlightened activity of power or overpowering external forces that can not be famed through the first two activities for example removing obstacles to sickness, ultimately death etc and forcefully accumulating conducive conditions for ones Dharma practice.

Black Tara sadana represents the enlightened activity of wrath which involves using forceful method for accomplished through other means.

Tara swift and Heroic function is to control and there is a ceremony in which a practitioner involves this Tara to turn back the power of others.

Jamyang Khyentse wagnpo says the White pacifying tara protects from general decline in the world and beings adversity attack from both physical and immaterial beings all sickness will influence, curses , black magic, strife and conceptual thinking.

Vajra Tara represents the protector of earth she protect from earthquake and avalanche in the outside world as well as inner sidness and evil influence caused by the negative emotion pride.

Meditating Red Tara she protects against harm from water she protects from all harm from water in the outside world including flooding shipwreck, polluted drinking water and drawing as well as sickness and evil influence caused by the negative emotion desire.

Tara protects harm from fire in the outside world including wild life and arson as well as sidness and evil influence caused by the negative emotion of anger.

Tara protects harm from wind in the outside world storms caused by evil spirits as well as sickness and evil influence caused by the negative emotion of Jealousy.

Tara against protect harm from meteors lightening and Hallstroms. Tara protects from harm caused by evil spirits or curses in the form of meteors, hail storms and lightning violent rainstorms and snow damage as well as sickness and evil influence caused by the negative emotions of desire hatred and envy.

Forest God Tara protect harm from weapon wind, fire, elephants, Lions, snakes etc. Lord Tara protect from attacks by fierce and powerful animals, elephants, horses, buffaloes and domestic wild animals Tara protect attacks by tigers, leopards, bears, Jackals in the outside world. Tara protects from attack by vipers, spiders, scorpions, rabid dogs, and other kinds of poisonous creatures.

Ma Tara protects from imprisionment and punishment by rulers , governors in the outside world-Tara protects from robbery, theft and murder in the outside world.

Tara protect the mind and physical body. She protects three type of evil spirits in the outside world.

Tara protects all kind of black magic curses, spells, epidemics and all evil forces, material as immaterial.

Tara protect against harm from disease she specifies sickness and maintaining a spritual life-Tara protect against fear of death, poverty and Failure

CHAPTER 6

PRAISE TO TARA

Tara protects from decline in prosperity, economy. Tara is a success creator.

Praises To the 21 Taras.

Who need protection enter beneath your right hand mudra of granting boons, the refuge mudra and be relieved from every fear.

Homage to Tara, swift and courageous who dispels all fears by TRUE with the syllables of homage SOHA bow to you.

1. Tara swift and courageous whose gaze is as quick as a flash of lightning who on a tear from the face of the protector of the 3 worlds Arose from a billion fold lotus pistill.

2. White Tara. Whose face is like a gathering of one hundred autumn full moons, who like a cluster of a thousand stars, Blazes light illuminating everything.

3. Golden Tara, adorned by a lotus , whose hand is holding a golden blue lotus perseverance, fortitude and giving , patience and samadhi are the scope of her action.

4. Yellow Tara who moves in endless victory-The crown Jewel of the Tathagates. Having obtained all transcendent virtues- The sons of the jinas take her support.

5. Hamsavardhini Tara who by the syllables TUT-TARE and HUNG fills all space, directions and realms of desire while trampling the seven worlds under her feet. she brings all and control everything.

6. Tariloka vijaya Tara whom indra, agni and vishesh-vara all worship, ghosts , zombies, ghandarvas, gonas and yakshas.

7. Arya padmini Tara who by TRAT and PAAT van-quishes evil forces and black magic. Right leg bent, ex-tended left leg trampling. she destroys them completely with intense blazing fire.

8. Mara sudha Tara, the swift fear some one who vanquishes the most tenacious of maras. When she knife her brows on her lotus face, she defeats all ene-mies without exception.

9. Varadha Tara, whose finger adorn your heart with the gesture of the sublime precious Three, Adorned with a wheel striking all directions without exception with the totality of your own rays of light.

10. Tara dispeller of sorrow who sparking garland of lights on her crown with great peal of laughter from the syllables TUTTARE she brings demons and the world under her control.

11. Tara summouer of beings who can summon forth. The assembly of all earth's protectors by the

wrathful quake of the HUNG in her frown she completely liberates all destitute beings.

12. Mangalaloka Tara , whose crescent moon tara, and jewelled ornaments sparkle brilliantly who from amitaba a top her vast stream of hair, Floods forth immense rays of light.

13. Tara the Ripener for subdilling engulfed in a fire like the kalpa's end who sits in the midst of a wreath of flames. Right leg stretched and left leg bent, she defeats all enemies of those who rejoice when the dharma wheel turns.

14. Bhrikuyh Tara, who strikes the earth with her palms and crushes it mightily under her feet who by HUNG and her wrathful glare. Rules the beings of the seven fold worlds.

15. Maha santhi Tara who praises blissful, virtous and peaceful mother whose activity is nirvanas sphere of tranquility by the fawless expression of SOHA and OM greatest of evils.

16. Tara destroyer of attachment who smashes the bodies of the enemies that impression joy, illuminated by the awareness of HUNG arranged with in a Mantra of ten syllables.

17. sulcha sadhana Tara praises when she stamps her foot. Her seed in the form of the syllable HUNG shakes the three worlds and mount meru, mandara and vidhya.

18. Sithavijaya Tara praises her in whose hands is placed the one who bears deer mark in the shape of a

36

godly lake. she annuals every poison with the twice uttered TARA and the sound of PHAT.

19. Tara burver of suffering several by the rular of the host of deities, By gods and kinnaras. The dazzling brightness her armor of joy dispels all quarrels and night mares.

20. siddi sambhava Tara who like the full sun and moon whose two eyes shine with blazing light by TUTTARE together with HARA reeited twice, she eliminates even the vilest sickness.

21. Tara the perfector endowed with the power to perfectly pacify through the arrangements of the three syllables of suchness. The crowds of demons zombies and yakshas are suppressed by TRUE the supreme mother.

these are the praises with the root mantra,

in the courage of the third Turning of the wheel of Dharma Buddha shakyamuni gave many teachings on Tara with in the categories of outer Tara inner Tara and the Great perfection. All of these including the 21 praise became yearly popular in India. They were brought to Tibet in the 18th century at the time of Gurupadmasambhava gave many Tara Teachings to his heart students including king Trisong peutsen and wisdom dakini yekshe Tsogual who was her self an emanation of Tara.

There are many lineases of the 21 Taras including the traditions coming from suryagupta, Dipamkara Atisha, each of these lineases portray the manifestations of Tara in different mantras and methods of practice. The

21 Taras depicted here follow the tradition of suryagupta who was one of the 84 mahasiddhas.

The 21 emanations of Tara,the mother of all the Buddhas manifest swiffly to protect sentient beings from all fears pacify evils, disease and misfortune increase longevity, wealth and merit , over power the deluded perception and destroy the enemies of five poisons ones disturbing emotions.

CHAPTER 8

Vajra kilaya Temple

This is the Temple of vajrakumara a deity representing enlightenment activity and the wrathful manifestation of vajrasattva. The monks from the junior High school and the pratsang perform a particular ritual in the temple daily specifically for the welfare of all sentient beings.

Vajra kilaya is the yidam deity who embodies the enlightened activity of all the buddhas and whose practice is famous for being the most powerful for removing obstacles, destroying the forces hostile to compassion and purify the spiritual pollution so prevalent in this age.vajra kilaya representing enlightened activity is vajra kilaya in peaceful form vajrakilaya considered as a very specific yogic use not merely considered an external deity to be worshipped in ritual activities.

vajrakumara is shown in teritic union with his wisdom prajnya consort, together they represent the union of wisdom and method which is active compassion. His five skilled crown represents the five addictions transmulated into the five wisdoms.

The vajrakilaya Tantric system is a yoga Tantra of Naingmoupa tradition of Tibetan Buddhism.All the Four Noble Truths the Buddha taught in his enlightement the recognition that every living being experiences suffering the recognition that it the causes are removed there will be an end to the suffering and the path or methods by which to achieve liberation from suffering or fill enlightenment.

The Buddhist Tantric teachings include methods for the purification of the psycho physical with in a pure environment or mandala. The details who inhabit a mandala are not external gods; rather they symbolize the enlightened state which everyone has the potential to realize

vajra kilaya is a warthful fierce deity symbolizing the energy needed to overcome and purify negative starts of mind.All the 21 Taras residing in the outer part of the mandala are fierce protector datails who ward of the interferences or distractions which might hinder the meditator. The meditator practicing Tantra one would familiarize one self with every detail of the mandala and the deities within it engaging in repeated exercises based upon visualizing the pure beings and pure environment which symbolize one's own being environment in purified , sumline form such excercises carried out with in the basic Buddist from work of developing wisdom and compassion bring about a profound transformation of the psyche.

Dzomgsar Khyentse Rinpoche on the practice of vajrakilaya states that vajrakilaya or kila means something sharp and something that pierces a dagger-A dagger that is so sharp it can pierce anything while at the quality This sharp and piercins energy is what is used to practice and out of the many infinite endless vajrayana methods this happens to be one of the most important methods.

vajrayogini is often described with the epithet sarava-buddha dakini meaning the dakini who is the essence of all Buddhas. Dakini is also conflated with ugra Tara. vajrayana teaches that the two stages of the practice of vajrayogini were originally taught by vajradhara -the instructions on the practice of ugra Tara contain concise and clearly presented meditations that are relatively essay to practice. The ugra tara and the body mandala are simple compared with those of other highest yoga Tantra. The practice of vajrayogini quickly brings blessings especially during this spirituality degenerate age. It is said that as the generated level of spirituality. decreases, it becomes increasingly difficult for practitioners to receive the blessings of other DETAILS Focussing initially on visual artists dancers and misicians creating in new forms and medicins we also feature galleries on traditional art highlighting 21 Taras and dakinis in meditational paintings.

women are the majority of devotees and meditations in the world presently her time is now and she is blossoming- A long awaited and necessary prtal of recognition and the praise of her many forms and how these are arising in new contexts as the Buddha dharma spreads around the globe.

dakini is the inner teacher the inner guru the fiery truth in our belly the force that guids us to move forward with fearlessness and compassion and to speak truthfully and with kindness.

CHAPTER 9

TARA THE VALUE CREATOR

Value systems are prospective and prescriptive beliefs ; they affect ethical behaviour of a person are the basis of universal meditation activities. Maa Tara create ethical value and economic value. value can be defned as broad preferences concerning appropriate courses of actions out comes . As such values reveals individuals sense of right and wrong what "ought" to be "Equal rights for all . Devotees should be treated with respect and loyalty are representatives of values. Tara influence attitudes and behaviour etical value for creating world peace.

A culture is a social system that shares a set of common values. Cultural values permit social expectations and collective understanding of the good and beautiful. personal value provide an internal reference for what is good benefical important, useful, beautiful desirable and influence the choices made by a person.

Management studies value can be defined self respect ,warm relationships fun and enjoyment excitement sence of belonging being well respected and security . Maa Tara cultural identity of a individual .value of society can often respect recieved by various groups and ideas . Tara encourages student to define their Own values and understand others values. There by ensure moral education.

21 Tara represents values defferently and to different levels of emphasis .Tara create value system . valu system is a set of consistent values . used for the purpose of ethical or ideological.

Tara prayer practice create economic value. It is generally measured by Wealth returns from goods and services. Maa Tara creating economic theyory of value. Consumer surplus can be converted in to social wealth. All the value is linked to price through the mechanism of exchange value in the most basic sense can be referred to as real value or Actual value. The theory of value is closely related to that to that of allocative efficiency, the quality by which firms produce those goods and services most valued by society.

Tara the protecter of economy ,efficiency and effectiveness there by ensuring equity and universal peace.

Tara the creator of cultural universal are found in all human societies. Art, music, dance, ritual, religion, technologies, architecture .science situated with in the set of knowledge acquired over time.

Tara the developer of civilization has often been under stood as multiculture and more advanced . Tara worship create civilization to society. Civilization also refers to the process of a society developing in to a centralized, urbanized, clear defined structure. Civilization concentrates power, extending human control over the rest of nature including over the human being.

Tara create interpersonal relationships with people human being respond in relationship, depend Tara worship. She protect them from loved ones or perceiving a threat. She is a care given all child become attached .Tara is familar care giver she provide protection and emotional support Maa Tara is the primary care giver for the childs successful social and emotional development child care and related social interaction. The mother child relation shows that Tara is The great mother and care taken of   all human kind. Mother Tara give emotional support and protection children fell their need fullfillment. Tara provide anxiuos ambivalent and anviodant attachment to children . When the orphen child,parent issues Tara been care taker Tara. worship related with all human kind attachment as a mother when adults feel close attachment to their parents, Tara protect fear of danger separation, sadness and despair if there is a greeting when the mother Tara enters it is tend to be a mere look or smile. Tara create reunion and protect ignoring, turning away as i like a parent. Mahasanthi Tara who protect the human kind.

Mangalaloka Tara who protects love and life. She support inner circle relationship such as respect , confiding reassurance sick care health , worries. There by ensure secure attachment to all human kind. Tara by ensure adults to intimaey approval and responsiveness from partners and protect healthand mind and avoid mistrust, sepration, anxiety. Face to face conversation to Tara develop self fullfilling. Mother Tara forming close relationship and maintaining emotional closness with the people.

Ugra Tara avoid mis understanding ,practicing mutu-al initiation and enjoyment of sex. Tara protect relation-al lossess death, rejection infidelity, abandonment.

The path of Buddha is truly one of balance and dig-inify . The mysore golden temple represents Buddha shakyamuni, The princely ascetic achieved the state of the Buddha in the dence jungles that one surround-ed .Gaya in present day Bihar at a place that is now called Bodgaya. Prince sidhartha set out to search for an everlasting solusion to the end the cycle of birth and death that has tormented all beings from time imme-morial after many year of serious meditation practice he attained Enlightment under Bodhi Tree Bodh gaya .He announced his acheivement to his five fellow ascet-ics,whom he had left in issipattan modern day saranath.

The thought of Budha are so dynamic .The prac-tice of non violent conduct and the cultivation of com-passion etc are universal tool for world peace. Budha revealed the Truth. The truth cures our diseases and re-deems us from perdition . The truth strengthness us in life and in death the truth alone can conquer the evil of error.

Namdrolling nyingmapa monastery was built accord-ing to the Architectural tradition of Tibet . Located in Bylakuppe. The statu to the right of Budha shakyamu-ni is depictiion of Gurupadma sambhava .also known as guru rinpoche was the 8 th century Budhist master from indian padmasambhava is the religious myth and ritual. According to sam van schaik padmasaam bhava introduce tantric buddism in to Tibet. He is regarded as

45

the founder of Nyingma Tradition . He had five main female Tantric companions beginning in india before his time in Tibet. He spreading dharma through out the religion .five emanation, kalasiddi for the activity emanation are the companions of guru.

The statue to the left of Buddha is that of Amitayus. The Bhudha of long life. Amitayus protect from evil ,violence and demonic harm, bringing long life to devotees and bestowing blessings on the places. Where the statue are positioned. Golden temple also become powerful supports for practicing Dharma ,Each of the golden statues are the memmories of great Budha masters. seeing these statues genuine worshippers get peace wisdom, kindness, compassion in minds.

Amithabha means infinite life , Amitayus also known as the Budha of immeasurable light and life. The basic doctrines concerning Amitabha and his vows are found in three canonical madhyana text infinite life sutra, amitayurdhyana sutra ,amitabha sutra. Through prossessing happiness. Amitabha is the center of a number of mantras in vajrayana practices.

Stupas serve as symbols of enlightment mind Representing the body speech and mind of the Buddhas along with many other auspicious afterings.

Prayer wheels in a clock wise direction with faith and devition there are millions of mantras and dharanis. prayer wheels path beings more than 1,300 small prayer wheel and 19 large ones.

For future generation study and value creation purpose the wall painting shows us that all that lives, whether they

Are plants, animals and human beings, Harmoney nature ecological balanced system etc .reveal the pictures. Wall painting around the temples are the four great kings the six sybols of longevity, the four harmonious friends,the wheel existence. All the paintings shows human animals plants harmoney inorder to ensure peace happiness ,truth prosperity in the world.

The truth is the end and aim of all existence and the worlds originate so that the truth may come and well there in accoring to aspirre for the truth for all things will pass away but the truth abide the forever.

worship of Tara Teach us truth . Truth is the above the power of death. Truth is the essence of life. Truth is a straight path for loving all the Tara are wonderful and glorious. They reveal to us the path of life . The truth is our hope and comfort.

The Buddha said "three things 0 disciples are characterized by secrecy love affairs ,priestly wisdom and all aberrations from the path of the truth.

A woman of the world is anxious to exibit her form and shape whether walking standing sitting or sleeping even Tara represented as a picture Tara protect to all kind of beings.

The changing things there is a constancy of law and when the law is seen there is truth . The truth lies hidden in samsara as the permanent in its changes.

The consciousness of self dims the eyes of the mind and hides the truth . It is the germ of evil .All living creatures are what their past actions made them for the law of cause and effect is uniform and without exception. The truth is a living power for good . The Tara has found the truth and the truth has been proclaimed by the lord Tara .

The glory of the world is like a flower .it stands in like a flower .It stands in full bloom in the morning and fades in the morning and fades in the heat of the day . Truth is the immortal part of mind .The truth of Tara well in your hearts .Trust in truth that love the truth that love the truth for the country of right is founded up on earth .the darkness of error is dispelled by the light of truth . Self is the beginning of all hatred inequity self is evil the creator of mischief self create selfishness. There is no evil but what flows from self. There is no wrong but what is done for general .The mother Tara beholding her child and the commotion which his birth created felt in her timorous heart .Tara mind is the source of others is easily noticed but that of one self is difficult to perceive speak the truth do not yield to anger Tara possess virtue and intteligence .who is just speaks the truth and does dharma,karma -The world will hold clear.

Truth is the reality and fact. Tara protect from falsehood . She can also suggest a logical factual or ethical meaning. Buddha view the concept of truth as basic .Tara worship we study truth involves both the quality of faithfulness, fidelity, loyalty, sincerity, veracity and that of agreement with reality.